DANGEROUSLY DRIVEN

DEBORAH BLAKE

Dangerously Driven

Deborah Blake

Cover art by earthlycharms.com

Interior design by Crystal Sarakas

OTHER FICTION BY DEBORAH BLAKE

Novels

WICKEDLY DANGEROUS

WICKEDLY WONDERFUL

WICKEDLY POWERFUL

DANGEROUSLY CHARMING

DANGEROUSLY DIVINE

DANGEROUSLY FIERCE

VEILED MAGIC

VEILED MENACE

VEILED ENCHANTMENTS

REINVENTING RUBY

Novellas

WICKEDLY MAGICAL

WICKEDLY EVER AFTER

WICKEDLY SPIRITED

To my family, both the one I was born to and the one I created. You all make my journey worth taking.

ACKNOWLEDGMENTS

As always, many people pitched in to help this book get to my wonderful readers. Huge thanks go out to Judy Levine, Karen Buys, and Skye Hughes for editing and proofreading, and to Crystal Sarakas and Sierra Newburn for formatting and general feedback assists.

And a big thank you to my readers for still wanting more of these stories!

CHAPTER ONE

THE SMELL OF DAMP EARTH FILLED MIKHAIL'S NOSTRILS AS the underground passageway narrowed even further. His flashlight's beam flickered and dimmed. He was fairly certain his heartbeat was stuttering in a matching rhythm. Mikhail hated caves. Gods, how he hated caves.

Damn it. Another dead end. The dying light showed him nothing but a blank wall made up of unforgiving stone and clay. He'd have to back out and try again. The sound of his labored breathing echoed in his ears. A scraped spot on one hand burned as he brushed it against the low ceiling, trying not to bump his head.

Finally, he was back in the tunnel he'd started out in. At least the roof was a little higher there, although that did nothing to lessen the weight of the rocks above him. *No choice. Had to take the other way, hope it would lead him where he needed to be. He had to go on, no matter how much he wanted nothing more than to bolt for the surface. The air. The sun.*

His flashlight gave one more unsteady flicker and died altogether, leaving him alone in the dark.

This was really not the reunion he'd been hoping for.

"I'm not doing it," Alexei said, putting his empty beer mug down on the scarred wooden bar in a way that was supposed to both indicate that the topic was closed and suggest that he was ready for a refill. Predictably, Bethany chose to ignore both.

"Why not?" she asked in a reasonable tone as she handed a gin and tonic over to a customer and then tucked the money into the till with the ease of long practice. "These are your brothers we're talking about, after all. And you haven't seen them for what, two years?"

"Almost three," Alexei said. He blinked, a bit startled to realize it had been that long. But hell, they'd traveled together for centuries before the disaster that separated them. What were three years? "No big deal."

Bethany narrowed her eyes. "Maybe it wasn't a big deal when you were all immortal," she said in a low voice. This was clearly going to be one of those conversations that neither of them would want to explain to the patrons. Of course, at almost midnight on an early May Thursday before the start of Cape Cod's tourist season, that meant about five people, all locals who had learned to more or less ignore the giant, bearded, leather-clad Alexei.

"But you don't have forever anymore. Don't you think it's time for the three of you to get over whatever it is that's holding you back, and get together again? I know you miss them."

That much was certainly true. Back when they were the Riders, whose job it was to protect and serve the legendary Baba Yagas, they spent more time together than apart. But their torture at the hands of the mad witch Brenna had broken their bodies, their spirits, and their bonds as brothers. They had all eventually managed to mend the first two, but none of them seemed able to cross the chasm that was the third. Clearly Bella was attempting to do that for them. But Alexei didn't know if he was ready.

"Maybe in a few months," he said. "Or, you know, when tourist season is over come September."

Bethany tapped one finger on the piece of heavy bond paper he was currently brooding over. "Bella didn't invite you to come in September. She invited you to come next week. In writing. On fancy paper, even. With the words 'please come' written in bold and underlined. I've never met the woman, but from your stories, it doesn't sound as though the Baba Yagas are prone to asking for frivolous favors. Maybe this isn't about you and the other Riders, did you ever think about that? Maybe there is some other reason she asked you to visit."

Alexei scowled in her general direction. That was a great theory, but he could tell when the Baba Yagas were up to something. The invitation might have come from Bella, but it said, "Please join me, Barbara, and Beka at my home in Wyoming." Why else would Bella want them all there if not to force a reunion between stubborn men who hadn't been able to manage it on their own?

"How about another beer?" he asked. He nudged the empty mug gently, in case she hadn't noticed his current existential crisis.

"How about you don't try and change the subject?" responded the love of his life, but she got him another beer anyway. Which was only one of the many reasons she was the love of his life. Nonetheless, his brother Gregori thought it was amusingly suitable that after thousands of years of drinking and brawling, Alexei had ended up falling for a pint-sized Scottish barmaid (and soon-to-be lawyer) with a temper and stubborn nature that matched his own.

"It's going to get busy soon," Alexei said. "You'll need me here."

"I like that you think that," Bethany said, patting him on the hand. "Considering that your idea of 'help' mostly involves taking up precious space on a stool and drinking up the profits. Although I confess, it is occasionally nice to have you around to carry something heavy from the back room." She grinned at him to show she was kidding (mostly), and tossed her red hair back over her shoulders. "Besides, I've got my Da around if I need a hand. That new electric wheelchair makes it a lot easier for him to get around, and he can still pull a pint with the best of them."

They both looked across the room where Calum McKenna was sitting with one of his old fishing buddies, looking as craggy and crabby as ever as they argued over some old dispute.

"Uh huh," Alexei said. "I can see how helpful he's being. Really, I think I should stay here, instead of gallivanting all over the country."

"Wyoming is hardly all over the country," Bethany said, rolling her eyes. It was a look he got often. And usually deserved. "What is it, two thousand miles from here? You used to do that at the drop of a hat when one of the Baba Yagas wanted you for something. Unless you were exaggerating when you told me all those stories." The corner of her mouth crooked up, as if daring him to admit to stretching the truth about his previous adventures.

He grunted at her, staring down into the depths of his beer as if its amber liquid held the answers to his questions. He might have exaggerated one or two of his feats (although not by much, since they were already pretty impressive), but he'd been accurate enough about the extent of his travels. Cape Cod to the outskirts of Douglas, Wyoming was nothing, comparatively speaking. Especially not when one was mounted on an enchanted steed-turned-Harley Davidson motorcycle that could go faster than any conventional bike and never needed gasoline.

"It's about that, I suppose," Alexei said, stroking his brown beard. "I could probably be there in a couple of days. But that's not the issue."

Bethany shook her head, then hopped up onto the bar, swung her legs over, and landed next to him on the other side. He'd seen her make that move a time or two when she was in a hurry to break up a bar fight, and found it inexplicably sexy. Despite his dour mood, it still made him smile. As did the kiss she planted on his lips once she'd crossed the space between them. Her soft mouth lingered for a moment on his before she pulled away.

"What exactly *is* the issue, then? You know I'll be fine, the bar will be fine, even the dogs will be fine, although I'm sure they'll miss you terribly." Alexei had helped her with a pregnant Great Dane she'd been fostering when they met, and then insisted on keeping two of the puppies, which were currently wrecking the house and chewing on everything. Luckily, Alexei had developed the ability to speak to animals, so he could tell them what they were doing wrong. Not that they listened.

"Lulu will probably pine," Alexei insisted, although it was more likely to be the reverse. "You know how she adores me."

"She adores the extra treats you sneak her when you think I'm not looking," Bethany said with a fake frown. "And I adore you too, but I think I'll survive a few days without you, as long as you promise to come back when you're done."

"Of course I'll come back," Alexei protested. "I'd never abandon my puppies!"

Bethany punched him in the shoulder, then shook out her hand. "Ow. I've got to remember not to do that." Her expression softened. "What are you afraid of, Alexei? You're not still convinced you let them down, just because your immense strength couldn't save them from that crazy former Baba, are you? Because nobody else thinks that. I'm sure that when you are all together again, it will seem just like old times."

"That's the thing, Beth," Alexei said, his voice so low she had to lean in to hear him. "It won't be the same. It will never be the same again." His chest ached at the very thought of it, in a familiar way no amount of beer could ease.

She sighed, putting one arm as far around him as it

would reach and giving him a hug. "Oh, babe, that's life. Things change. My father fell off a roof and broke his back and he'll never be a fisherman again, or be able to run *The Hook and Anchor* without help. I had planned to stay in Boston after I finished my law degree, and now I'll be working out of a bar in Cape Cod and slinging drinks when I'm not helping the locals with their legal problems. But my dad is doing better, thanks to your stubborn insistence, and I've got you, which is a gift I never expected."

She kissed him again, a little harder than the first time as if to be sure she had his attention, then stared into his eyes. "Things have changed for you and your brothers. I get that it is hard for you to adjust to such a large difference, after so many years of your lives remaining essentially the same even when the world shifted around you. But they're still your brothers, and you are going to have to find some way to make your peace with the new reality. You know what would be a good start on that?"

Alexei gave her a wry grin. Bethany might be half his size, but she still won most of the arguments. "A nice trip to visit Bella in Wyoming?"

Bethany grinned back and took a swig of his beer. "I'll help you pack when we get home."

"No, I do not believe I will go," Gregori said, in answer to Ciera's question. "I think it unlikely that my brothers will attend either. It is a kind gesture on Bella's part, but unnecessary. Mikhail, Alexei, and I will reunite when the time is right. It is clear Alexei is simply not ready yet."

His wife raised one dark eyebrow. "I'm not sure Alexei is the only one who isn't ready," she said in a dry tone. "After all, you're not exactly going out of your way to spend time with your brothers either."

Gregori gently removed their black cat Magic from the counter, where she wasn't allowed, so he could put the next stack of dishes into the soapy water of the sink. He found washing dishes to be a soothing labor, probably a habit left over from his time spent in a Buddhist monastery. At the time he had been trying to find peace and balance in an effort to get a handle on his out-of-control new healing and precognitive abilities. Thankfully, another alternative had presented itself, since he clearly was not cut out to be a monk.

"I saw Mikhail at our wedding," Gregori reminded Ciera. He still found it hard to believe that after more than a thousand years of endless travel, he had been fortunate enough to end up with this wonderful woman. He found it very satisfying to spend his days helping her to run the *Blue Skies Center for At-Risk Youth* that she had founded in memory of the mentor who saved her from a life on the streets. It was important for him to have a life of service, even if it was not the one he had been born to live.

"At the summer solstice," Ciera reminded him back. "That was last June and now here it is May, and you haven't seen each other since."

"Well, we have been busy getting the Center up and running, not to mention my teaching classes in self-defense and meditation to the teens. There has not been much free time for travel." Even to his own ears, it sounded as though he was making excuses. Ciera obviously agreed.

"Mikhail is in upstate New York. That's hardly Timbuktu," she said. "You could easily have taken a couple of days to go see how he, Jenna, and little Flora are doing. And Bella's house in Wyoming isn't that far from us here in Minneapolis, either. Your shiny magical red Ducati could have you there in no time. So what's the real problem?"

Gregori pondered the question in silence for a moment. Ciera let him take his time; she knew him well enough to have learned that he was more inclined to intense thought than rapid responses.

"I am…concerned," he said, finally, placing the last dish in the stainless steel rack by the sink and sitting down at the small kitchen table.

Ciera pulled up a chair and sat next to him, her kinky-curly black hair shining under the overhead light. "Concerned about what? Have you had some kind of premonition about the gathering?" Tiny frown lines appeared on her forehead. There had been a time when his unexpected new powers had almost killed him, although these days he had them mostly under control, thanks to intensive lessons with his mother, an ancient and powerful shamaness.

He squeezed her hand, then held on to it, although he could not be sure if it was for her comfort or for his.

"No, nothing like that. It is simply that the last time we were all together, it was under such terrible circumstances. We barely survived being tortured by Brenna, and she stole our immortality in a futile attempt to extend her own life and powers. At the time, our connection as brothers was all that enabled us to hold on, but once it was over, each of us felt we had let the others down. Mikhail and I have been able to get past that, for the most part, but it is clear that Alexei still cannot forgive himself. Or perhaps, us."

"Is that what you're afraid of?" Ciera asked. "That he will blame you? Because as far as I can tell, that's never been the issue. You said when he called you last March he was blaming himself for not being strong enough to stop one small, ancient witch." Her full lips curved up slightly. "You know, kind of like you blamed yourself for not being able to outsmart her."

Gregori found himself smiling back at her; she often

had that effect on him. "You make it sound so foolish when you put it like that."

"Go figure," Ciera said dryly. "Maybe you should just go and see who else shows up. After all, Bella did ask you to come, and it seems to me that even if you aren't a Rider anymore, you owe her the courtesy of a visit when she requests one. Maybe this has something to do with what happened to her adopted daughter Jazz. They've both been off in the Otherworld for most of the last year, since that spell went really wrong. Maybe they need your support."

Gregori was ashamed he had been so focused on his own issues, he had not even considered that possibility. "It is not my place to support the Baba Yagas any longer," he pointed out, but with less conviction than his initial statement.

Ciera gazed at him steadily. "Circumstances beyond your control took away your ability to be a Rider," she said. "Nobody said you couldn't be a friend."

Or a brother. Gregori had the sneaking feeling that he had just lost an argument he had not been aware he was having.

"I am a fortunate man, to have such a wise wife," he said, leaning over and kissing her.

"Yes you are," she said with a smirk as she tugged on his long black hair. "And if you follow me to the bedroom, I'll show you just how lucky you are."

"I don't think either of them is likely to come," Mikhail said to his wife Jenna. He juggled Flora on his knee, feeling his heart lighten at the sound of her high-pitched giggle. Her dark locks hung in wild curls that bounced on her shoulders as he made silly horsy sounds, her tiny hand gripping his own shoulder-length blond hair with a hold of iron.

Three years ago, a moment like this would have been impossible for him to imagine. A lot had happened in those three years. Some of it very, very bad, and some of it incredibly good. In balance, he mostly thought he'd come out a winner. Except for the continued absence of his brothers, his life was pretty good. A lot more limited in time than it had been, but pretty good nonetheless.

"What makes you think they won't come?" Jenna asked, putting supper on the table and then plucking Flora out of his arms to plop the eighteen-month old into her high chair. "You're usually such an optimist. What's with the pessimism?"

"Titten nunnets!" Flora said gleefully. "Dada, Titten nunnets!"

Mikhail felt a smile tug at the corners of his mouth. Chicken nuggets (in this case, made from organic chickens raised by their neighbors, not some nasty chem-ical-laced thing from the freezer case at the store) were

Flora's favorite food. But that wasn't what made him smile. He still lit up with joy every time the small girl called him dad. He wasn't her biological father—that honor went to a jerk named Stu who had treated Jenna like crap—but Mikhail had been there literally since before Flora was born, and in his heart, she was definitely his child.

That was a title he'd never thought to aspire to, since the Riders, as the immortal children of a god and three different not-strictly-Human mothers, couldn't have children. At least so far as they knew. Their father had never said, specifically. But it had never happened in thousands of years, so that seemed likely to be the case.

Mikhail missed his role as a Rider—missed it as a deep ache in his soul every day—but his role as father and husband more than almost made up for it.

Maybe that was why he had made a better adjustment to his new life than either of his brothers, although Gregori, who Mikhail talked to occasionally, seemed to be finding his path. Alexei, well, Alexei he wasn't so sure about. Beka, the Baba Yaga who was usually in charge of the western third of the country, had worked with Alexei on a paranormal issue a couple of months ago in Cape Cod, and swore that he was doing better now. But if that was true, why hadn't he been in touch?

"I'm not being pessimistic, exactly," Mikhail said, dragging his head back into the conversation. "Just realistic. It has been a long time since all three of us were together. First, we hid out in separate corners of the Otherworld to heal. Then we set out on different paths to try and find out who we were if we couldn't be Riders any more. I'm worried that the more time that passes, the harder it will be for us to come back together."

To be honest, he was starting to worry it would never happen. But the thought of spending the rest of his life without his brothers made his heart feel as though it was being squeezed by a giant, a spasm of intense pain almost greater than he had suffered when being tortured by the most vicious person he had ever met. He couldn't even form those words out loud, for fear that would make them come true.

"All the more reason to go to Bella's house," Jenna said firmly.

"Oh, he's going, all right," a strong tenor voice said from the doorway. A tall woman with a cloud of dark hair stepped into the kitchen as though she belonged there. Which she did, really. "I hope you don't mind. I let myself in when you didn't hear my knock. I didn't mean to interrupt your dinner."

Mikhail grinned at her. "Although you would have anyway, even if you had known." Barbara Yager waited for no man. Or meal. "Here, take a seat. There's plenty."

Having one of the Baba Yagas as a neighbor would also have seemed impossible three years ago, since neither the witches nor their companion Riders had been the type to settle down. Barbara still periodically traveled around the eastern third of the United States in her enchanted silver Airstream trailer (her version of the updated hut on chicken's legs) with her dragon Chudo Yudo disguised as a giant white pit bull. When she wasn't on the road, she lived in the yellow farmhouse she shared with her husband and adopted daughter Babs, a miniature Baba Yaga in training.

When Mikhail and Jenna got together at the end of a long and very strange adventure and needed to find a place to raise Flora, it seemed only natural to settle in next door to Barbara, Babs, and Liam, a Human sheriff who had somehow tamed the untamable mythical witch. As a result, Mikhail had stayed in touch with all the Baba Yagas—Barbara, Bella, and Beka—and had a better idea of what had been going on than either of his brothers likely had. She was right. There was no way he was going to miss this gathering.

He hoped his brothers would defy his expectations and show up, but either way, he wouldn't miss it for the world. He was only sorry that Jenna and little Flora weren't coming too. But the invitation was for Baba Yagas and former Riders only.

"Not to worry," he assured Barbara. "I can't wait to see how things have worked out with Jazz. I still can't believe she and Bella have had to spend more than a year in the

Otherworld. I'm sure Sam is happy to have them back full time instead of for quick visits."

"We all will be," Barbara said firmly. She and Beka had been covering Bella's territory as well as their own since the High Queen had decreed that Jazz undergo an intensive magical training on the other side of the doorway between the worlds. Mikhail was sure they would all be relieved to have things back to normal. Or at least, as close to normal as they would ever get again. As always, the thought of what he'd lost made his stomach clench, but he'd learned to live with it. It hardly hurt at all anymore. Only three minutes out of every four.

"So, I'm planning to take the Airstream and Babs and Chudo Yudo and set out tomorrow," Barbara said. "We thought we'd get there a little early so I could catch Bella up on what's been happening in the middle of the country while she was gone. Plus, Babs has questions to ask."

Jenna and Mikhail both laughed at that; Babs *always* had questions to ask. She had been stolen from her Human parents as a baby, hidden away and raised in the Otherworld by Melissa, Liam's insane former wife. Not exactly the kind of start that produced a typical child.

When Barbara and Liam had rescued the little girl, the strange twists and turns of time in the Otherworld had aged that baby to about six years old in what had been less than a year on this side of the doorway. With her parents murdered, and no way to explain her rapid growth to any relatives who might have claimed her, it would have been impossible to bring her back as herself. Luckily, she showed strong magical abilities, and Barbara was able to convince the queen to allow the child to be trained as a Baba Yaga.

Babs was now about nine, a dark-haired, solemn, wide-eyed pixie of a girl who rarely spoke to strangers and was still a bit awkward with Human societal norms. But she was also bright and inquisitive and affectionate to those few people she allowed close to her, and not at all intimidated by living with a huge dog who was occasionally a small dragon. Or even by Barbara, who most people found at least a little bit scary, even if they didn't know why.

"Babs is going?" Jenna said. She handed Barbara a beer, which the tall woman accepted graciously. "I thought families weren't invited to this particular occasion."

She wasn't complaining, Mikhail thought. He knew perfectly well she'd rather stay home. His Jenna was plenty tough in her own right, but all three Baba Yagas together could be a little...overwhelming.

Barbara shrugged, snagging a chunk of lightly breaded chicken from the platter in the middle of the table. "Babs isn't just family; she's a Baba Yaga in training. This is Baba business, so she goes. But Liam will still be around if you need anything while we're gone." She nodded at Mikhail. "I thought I'd see if you wanted to catch a ride with us in the Airstream, save you the ride halfway across the country on your Yamaha."

Mikhail laughed. "Nah, it will actually be nice to take a little bit of a road trip on the old girl. It's not too bad— about eighteen hundred miles. It would probably take a little over two days of driving on a mundane bike, plus stops to rest, but my trusty steed Krasivaya can do it in a lot less if she puts her enchanted mind to it." Both the Riders' magic steeds-turned motorcycles and the Baba Yaga's enchanted ex-huts could bend time and distance in ways no one could quite explain. That made it faster and easier for them to get to problem areas when necessary. Very handy.

He turned and smiled at Jenna, enjoying the way she smiled back with a warmth she saved especially for him. "Besides, I don't want to be away from my ladies any longer than I have to be. So you go ahead, I'll be a couple of days behind you."

Barbara stared down her long nose at him and narrowed her amber eyes. "So long as you show up in time for the party."

"Wild horses couldn't keep me away," Mikhail promised. "I just wish…"

"I know," Barbara said. "We all wish that. Who knows, maybe Gregori and Alexei will surprise us." Her eyes twinkled. "Something tells me this get together might be full of surprises."

Uh oh. Mikhail had the sudden feeling he should brace himself. Baba Yagas and surprises were rarely a good combination.

CHAPTER TWO

THREE DAYS LATER, MIKHAIL WAS RIDING THROUGH
Nebraska, enjoying the somewhat stark scenery and the
bittersweet pleasure of the long drive that echoed so
many others he had taken before.

It still seemed strange not to have his brothers beside
him; Alexei on his huge black Harley, dressed head to toe
in black leather covered with silver chains, his braided
beard blowing in the breeze, and Gregori in his red
leathers perched on his matching red Ducati as they ate
up the miles with ease. The White Rider, the Black Rider,
and the Red Rider—figures out of Russian mythology to
most. It was hard to believe those days were over. But
Mikhail never wore white anymore. Never. Not now that
he was no longer the White Rider.

They had grown up spending part of the year with

their various mothers in different parts of Russia and the other part in the realm of the gods, far removed from earthly concerns. Their father, Jarilo, a relatively unimportant god in the Slavic pantheon, mostly ignored them, leaving the three half brothers to run wild through the mystical land where it was always summer. Gregori, the oldest, tried to instill some sort of order into their lives, but wild Alexei could almost always be depended on to lead them into trouble. He, Mikhail, the youngest, worshipped his older brothers, and spent much of his time charming treats for them all out of the palace cooks.

When they reached manhood, Jarilo sent them out to do the work for which they had been created, acting as companions, assistants, and occasionally brute muscle for the Baba Yagas who lived in the deep dark woods of Mother Russia. Over time, the Babas spread out to cover most of the known world, and other Riders were born to aid the newer additions.

The Babas aged (albeit slower than a normal Human, thanks to the elixir called the Water of Life and Death brewed for them by the High Queen) and retired and were replaced by other Babas. Only these Riders remained unchanged, eventually following three of the Baba Yagas of the original lineage when they left Russia and went to the New World.

Then a former Baba named Brenna decided she wasn't willing to give up the power and the magic, and hatched an insane plot to steal the Riders' immortality and make it her own. She failed, thanks to the other Baba Yagas and Koshka, Bella's dragon-cat. But by the time the men had been rescued, the damage was already done. Their charmed lives were over, and nothing would ever be the same again.

They had been created for one purpose, spent their very long lives serving that purpose to the best of their ability, and then one day, it was simply...gone. And it seemed that the ties that had bound them together were gone along with it.

Each of them had been wracked with guilt in the aftermath of Brenna's vicious torment. Mikhail, because he had allowed himself to be fooled by Brenna's ploy that used his weakness for a damsel in distress, since his capture had been used to lure the others into her trap. Alexei, because he thought his great strength should have been enough to protect his brothers and break them free, and Gregori, because he was the eldest and the wisest, and felt that he should have been able to outthink the deranged mind that held them.

In their guilt and grief and shock, they had all gone off alone to try and find a new purpose that would fill the now-limited days that remained. And they all had eventually discovered heretofore unknown paranormal abilities, probably inherited from their mothers and only allowed to surface once the more powerful influence of their father waned with the loss of their immortality. And they had all found love, as unexpected and unsought after as it had been wonderful.

But they hadn't yet found their way back to each other.

That was why Mikhail's drive, while beautiful, also carried with it pain and loss and grief, blurring his vision so much that he almost missed the nondescript old Ford that was pulled off to the side of the road, and the frantic woman standing next to it, waving him down.

For a moment, he hesitated. After Brenna, he'd sworn never to rescue a damsel in distress again. A vow he'd kept until one literally landed on his doorstep at a rented cabin deep in the woods of the Adirondacks, in the form of a pregnant woman on the run from a faery's curse. That woman had turned out to be Jenna, and the universe made it clear that he'd had no choice but to help, vow or no vow. Considering the way things had turned out, he couldn't regret that.

And he'd only caught a quick glimpse of the woman by the side of the road, but he was sure he'd seen a huge belly.

Mikhail slowed, feeling the quivers of his PTSD pricking at his nerves and making him twitch. But he turned the Yamaha around and rode back the way he'd come. He might not be a Rider anymore, or the Mikhail Day he had once been, but he'd be damned if he'd let the trauma from a bad experience keep him from coming to this woman's aid. It was highly unlikely it was some kind of magical trap, after all. He had nothing else for anyone to steal. And if it was? At least he would go out with no regrets.

"Oh, thank god," the woman said when he'd gotten off his bike and removed his helmet to let his long blond hair fall to his shoulders. "I been here for twenty minutes, and the only people I've seen just kept going." She was almost as fair as he was, with pale skin and a stomach that jutted far out in front of her otherwise slim body. Panic had etched lines around her blue eyes and sweat dotted her tense face.

"Did your car break down?" Mikhail asked in a gentle voice. He knew it was scary to be a woman alone in the middle of nowhere, and he tried his best to seem unthreatening. Since he was a big man with broad shoulders and muscular arms, that might have been tough, but he had always been charming, and he flashed her a low-wattage version of his "trust me, I'm harmless" smile.

Tears ran down her face. "No, the car is okay. I had to stop and pee," she patted her large belly. "I think the baby is resting right on top of my bladder." She shook her head, as if to rid it of the irrelevant fact. "Anyway, I dashed into the trees really quickly with my daughter Ella. She's two, almost three. And when my back was turned, she ran off down a path. By the time I caught up, she had fallen into a cave!"

The look of panic got even stronger, and her voice took on an edge of hysteria as she tried to explain, her breathing ragged and uneven. "I can hear her crying, but I can't climb down into the cave like this. There's no cell signal here, and for all I know she could be hurt, or even dying. You have to help me." She wrung her hands, tears pouring down like rain, her expression pleading. "Please. Please. You have to save my little girl."

Aw, hell.

It had to be a cave. Of course it did. He could almost hear the universe laughing.

Mikhail didn't have anything against caves, other than the fact that he never wanted to go into one again.

The very thought made him shudder. Brenna's cave stank of mold and fear, its floor and sides perpetually ran with moisture. He and his brothers were always cold, and after a while the walls seemed to close in around him, Alexei's and Gregori's screams echoing even when they were silent. Caves. He freaking *hated* caves.

Mikhail rotated his head to try to loosen up his shoulders, and took a deep breath. "I guess you'd better show me where it is," he said. "I'm Mick," by the way." He grabbed a flashlight out of one of the Yamaha's saddle-bags. The hand holding it gave a treacherous wobble, which he ignored by force of will.

"Louisa," the woman said, then led him down a barely visible trail, probably made by wildlife, since it was an unlikely spot for hikers.

"There," she said, stopping in front of a slanting hole that led underground. "She fell down there." She bent down and hollered, "Ella, Ella, can you hear me? It's mama!"

Mikhail thought he might have heard a thin wail in return, but it could have been the wind whistling through the hollow space if there was another place where it came out above ground. The hole was simply that—an empty spot in the woodland floor, like a gaping maw waiting to swallow up an unwary traveler. Or anyone stupid enough to go in after one.

He gave Louisa a cheerful smile. "Don't you worry; I'll bring her up for you." He paused. "But if we're not back in an hour, you might want to go for help. At least you'll know she's not alone down there." He eyed the cave entrance. It was relatively small and more oblong than round. Louisa was right; she never would have fit inside. As it was, he was going to have a tough time squeezing his large shoulders through without losing some skin.

Still, it wasn't as though there were any choice. He lowered his legs down into the emptiness, feeling around for a protrusion that might act as a step. When he found one, he slithered in, only to slip and fall the last few feet down into the belly of the earth. If he grabbed at the dirt as he fell, digging his nails in deep, that was only to steady the transition. Not because he was fighting the instinctive desire to lift himself right back out. Crawl out on his hands and knees, if that's what it took.

When his boots touched solid ground, the darkness was nearly complete, the entrance above merely a glimmer of light about ten feet overhead. He turned on the flashlight with hands that barely shook at all, fighting the desire to cover his ears against screams that this cave had never heard, to forget about the little girl waiting to be rescued and just climb toward the light and the air and freedom.

The flashlight flickered, and he almost sank to the dirt, his heart pounding so hard, he thought it would jump out through the faded denim shirt he wore. *No.* He would not let the past rule his future. He took a few deep breaths, as Gregori had taught him during the brief time they'd spent together after Mikhail's wedding.

Courage isn't the absence of fear, Mikhail reminded himself. *It's doing what you have to do even when you're afraid.* Right now, that didn't really help.

Then a few more breaths, until the earth felt steady under his feet again. The beam from the flashlight barely pierced the stygian darkness, enough to show him dirt walls and a ceiling barely higher than his own six foot three. Claustrophobia, his constant companion since the nightmare with Brenna, made his breath catch in his throat as the cave shrank in around him.

He kept moving anyway. The main cavern branched off in three directions. There was no sign to tell him which way the little girl had gone. Where was a nice trail of breadcrumbs when you needed one?

He turned left, for the lack of any better options, but that tunnel ended in a dead end before he'd gone more than a few yards. The beam from the flashlight waned, then grew stronger again as he struck it firmly against his palm. Stupid. What kind of Rider has a magical motorcycle and such an undependable source of illumination? An ex-Rider, he supposed. Still, it might be worth asking one of the Baba Yagas for something enchanted. If and when he ever made it out of this damned cave and to the destination at the end of his journey.

There was a reason he and his brothers hadn't let themselves be distracted by mundane Human affairs when they'd been traveling. Too many things could go wrong.

He returned to the central section and turned right. Was that a faint cry he heard? He bent over into a crouch as the ceiling grew lower and the walls grew closer, but he kept on moving.

The smell of damp earth filled Mikhail's nostrils as

the underground passageway narrowed even further. His flashlight's beam flickered and dimmed. He was fairly certain his heartbeat was stuttering in a matching rhythm. Mikhail hated caves. Gods, how he hated caves.

Damn it. Another dead end. The dying light showed him nothing but a blank wall made up of unforgiving stone and clay. He'd have to back out and try again. The sound of his labored breathing echoed in his ears. A scraped spot on one hand burned as he brushed it against the low ceiling, trying not to bump his head.

Finally, he was back in the tunnel he'd started out in. At least the roof was a little higher there, although that did nothing to lessen the weight of the rocks above him. *No choice. Had to take the other way, hope it would lead him where he needed to be. He had to go on, no matter how much he wanted nothing more than to bolt for the surface. The air. The sun.*

His flashlight gave one more unsteady flicker and died altogether, leaving him alone in the dark.

This was really not the reunion he'd been hoping for.

He wished he could see. Maybe then he wouldn't feel like an animal caught in a trap.

The thought ricocheted around in his head for a moment and he began to laugh. An animal would do far better under these circumstances. Luckily, that was something he knew a little bit about.

Around the time Jenna showed up at his door, strange

things had started happening to him. It had taken him a while to discover that when angered, he transformed into a large greenish bear-shaped creature. This was undoubtedly the heritage of his mother, one of the nearly forgotten legendary Lethy who lived in the deepest forests of Russia.

Gregori had theorized that the Lethy were distantly related to other similar "monsters," like the Sasquatch and Bigfoot, although no one really knew for sure. The Lethy could take on Human form, and eventually, working with Barbara, Mikhail learned to tame his inner beast so he could now control it, instead of having it take over. Ironically, he had focused most of his practice on working to suppress his ability to transform, but now he needed to find out if he could summon it at will. Desperately.

He forced himself to close his eyes, as vulnerable as that made him feel, and reached deep inside. Once he did, it was surprisingly easy to find his beast-self, almost as though it had been waiting for him. A shimmering greenish aura that hovered lightly inside the brighter light that was his more traditional energy field, it radiated a sense of restrained power and brute force.

Mikhail concentrated on bringing forth the aspects he needed—not the rage or fighting spirit, but rather the forest-dwelling gifts that would be most useful in this situation. When he reopened his eyes, his vision was sharper, picking out details in the dim light that even his normally keener-than-most perception had been unable to see. He could smell mold and tiny mammals and just a hint of something that didn't belong in this environment.

Looking down, he could make out long, green-tinged fur covering his body, and sharp claws on the hand holding the flashlight. He hoped he wouldn't scare the child, but at least now he had some hope of finding her.

Being in this form calmed his anxiety too. Perhaps because his previous traumatic experiences had happened, not to the beast, but to him alone. Perhaps it felt more at home underground than he did. Either way, he could finally draw in a deep breath. He would have stood up straight, but in creature form he was even taller than usual, so stooping slightly, he followed the scent he'd picked up, sniffing from time to time to make sure he didn't lose it.

The trail let down a narrow, meandering passageway past numerous turnoffs to a small alcove tucked into the cave wall; he wasn't sure if he would ever have found it in his (mostly) Human form. A tiny girl was curled up in the farthest corner, crying quietly and sucking her thumb. Perversely, the flashlight picked that time to spring back to life.

"Hello Ella," he said, the words only a little roughened by their transition through his beast's mouth. "My name is Mick. Your mother sent me to find you. Would you like to go see her now?"

In the flashlight's dim glow, he saw her nod. He wasn't sure if she could see well enough to make out the unusual shape of her rescuer, but she seemed to accept his presence and calmly put her tiny hand into his gigantic claw-tipped paw and allowed him to lead her back the way he'd come. Once they reached the space beneath the hole to the surface, where the light was somewhat brighter, Ella blinked at him.

"Are you a monster?" she asked.

Mikhail had been asking himself that same question since his creature-self first appeared. "No, Ella," he said. "I am just...different. But don't worry, I'm not going to hurt you. If you close your eyes, I will show you a magic trick. Would you like that?"

The little girl nodded earnestly and squeezed her eyes shut. Mikhail stifled a chuckle as he did the same, willing himself back into his own form. He breathed a sigh of relief when he looked down and saw denim-clad legs instead of fur.

"Okay," he said cheerfully. "You can open your eyes now."

Ella put her free hand over her mouth. "Oooh! Fun!"

"That's right," Mikhail said. "So much fun. Now let's get you back to your mama. She is very worried about you." *And that's without knowing you were in the cave with a huge hairy green beast...*

Louisa was beside herself with joy when Mikhail handed little Ella up out of the darkness, then climbed out after her. He brushed some dirt off his clothes and gave her a huge smile.

"Here we are," he said. "Safe and sound, and no worse for the experience. Will you be okay now?"

The woman nodded. "I don't know how to thank you. We would have been lost without you."

Mikhail shrugged. "Anyone else would have done the same," he said. But he hummed all the way back to his bike, happy to have been of use again. He had started a small private detective agency back in Clearwater County, mostly helping out in unofficial ways when Barbara's husband Liam couldn't do anything as sheriff. But it wasn't the same as being a Rider.

Mikhail had to confess, if only to himself, and to his trusty steed-turned-Yamaha, Krasivaya, that he kind of missed the hero business. It had been nice to feel like the White Rider again, even if only for a few minutes. And even if he had been green at the time.

CHAPTER THREE

GREGORI WAS SOMEWHERE IN SOUTH DAKOTA WHEN HE crossed the Lewis and Clark Memorial Bridge going across I-90. It was a basic and not very decorative structure, with low barriers on either side and two narrow lanes on each side running over the Missouri River. But he enjoyed the view of the water, which was unobstructed by the high railings featured on other, more modern bridges. It was running fast, deeper than usual with the last of the snow melt from mountains far away.

He had taken advantage of the lack of other vehicles to slow down, gazing at the wide expanse of river with pleasure, and barely noticed a teenage boy standing by the side of the bridge in a tee shirt and ragged jeans, a large knapsack propped up next to him.

Gregori wondered if the boy was hitchhiking, since

there was no sign of another car anywhere nearby. Still, it was none of his business, so he kept on going. Back in their days as the Riders, he and his brothers had learned to avoid getting involved in the affairs of Humans. Those people always had some problem that invited meddling and the Riders had other jobs to do.

The way the youth had been standing, though, reminded him of the at-risk teens at the Center. Those slumped shoulders and the discouraged droop of the head made Gregori wonder if the boy was a runaway. If Gregori had been in Minneapolis, he might even have stopped to give the kid a flier for the Center, but there didn't seem to be much point to doing so now.

He was still trying to persuade himself that he was probably fretting about nothing when the vision hit. So vivid it nearly blocked out the road in front of him, Gregori was suddenly grateful for his slow speed as he eased the Ducati to the edge of the highway.

He'd struggled with his precognitive abilities when they first appeared along with a gift for healing that had almost killed him when he'd used it without any control over the amount of energy it drained from him. Mostly these days the visions were mild—suggestions of possible futures, or hints from the universe that helped to guide his steps.

This one though, was a single clear image: the bridge he had just crossed, looking exactly the same, except that the knapsack sat alone on an otherwise empty stretch of road. A shudder ran down Gregori's spine.

Not my problem, he reminded himself. The bike's headlights were aimed down the road, in the direction he was supposed to be heading. It made no sense to stop and involve himself in every Human problem. He could not solve them all. Could not even make a dent. And yet...did not the Buddhist teachings he had studied say that every life was sacred? Certainly he had acquired an intimate knowledge of how fragile life could be, and how precious.

He changed his course, spinning the bike around and heading back the way he'd come. Just as he approached, he saw the teen climb over the side of the bridge and fling himself into the deep waters below.

Gregori screeched to a stop, trusting his enchanted motorcycle to take care of itself as he pulled off his black leather jacket and leapt off the bridge without a moment's hesitation. Hitting the surface of the water in a clean dive, Gregori still felt the impact like a hammer as the river closed over his head. He was pretty sure the river had been nearly thirty feet below the bridge—a long way for a Human to fall. Luckily, the Riders were still tougher than the average person, even without their immortality. It paid to have a god as a father.

Looking around, he could see the boy far below him, struggling feebly against the river's current. Gregori kicked strong legs in his direction, barely hampered by the drag from his wet clothes and heavy motorcycle boots. He grabbed the youth by his collar and scissor-kicked to the surface, relieved to hear sputtering and gasping from his companion as they broke through. Gregori had been afraid the boy would fight him, but once he struck out for shore, the teen allowed himself to be towed along, and collapsed on the bank with a sobbing sigh, clutching at the grass with both hands.

"Changed your mind, did you?" Gregori said in a mild, carefully nonjudgmental tone as he pulled himself into a sitting position. His hair, grown back into its original long black tail after he'd cut it short, dripped down his back as he took off his shirt, wrung it out, and put it back on.

The boy coughed up river water a couple of times before he could get out anything resembling words.

"Yeah," he said finally. "Just as soon as I could feel myself falling." He paused, and then added. "Thanks for coming in after me. That was kind of crazy."

Gregori smiled. "You are very welcome. And I suppose it was. But it seemed like the thing to do at the time."

They sat there in silence for a moment, both of them dripping onto the grass and staring out at the river in front of them.

"How did you know to come back?" the boy asked

after a while. "I know you couldn't see me, because I waited until you were out of view."

"Call it a gut feeling," Gregori said. "I work with people your age back home in Minnesota. Kids who are dealing with difficult situations, homelessness and drugs and abuse. Something about you reminded me of them." All true enough, although it left out the bit about the vision. That was probably best left out of the conversation.

"Oh," the boy said. "Minnesota. That's a long way away."

"It is," Gregori said. "And it is not. Distance is relative. So are problems, although it might be hard to believe that right now. Something that seems impossible to deal with today might appear much more manageable tomorrow. Or the day after tomorrow."

The boy looked at him sideways from underneath ragged, over-long bangs that clung to his thin face like seaweed. His whole body was narrow and scrawny, from his slender shoulders to the bony wrists and ankles that stuck out from underneath clothing a size too small for his frame. Gregori thought he looked about fourteen or fifteen, but he could have been older. It was hard to tell with the ones who had been through the wars.

"How would you know?"

"I have dealt with my own share of impossible todays,"

Gregori said. "And come out the other side when I was not sure I would."

The boy stared at him with doubt for a moment, but something in Gregori's voice must have rung true. "How? How do you get to the other side?"

Gregori patted him gently on the shoulder, then stood and offered the teen a hand up. "Stubborn persistence, a refusal to give in to the darkness, and if you are lucky, a good friend or two."

The boy shook his head, although he accepted Gregori's help up the rough incline towards the road. "I don't have any friends."

"Oh, I disagree," Gregori said. "I think anyone who dives into a river to save your life should count as one. And I can put you in touch with some people who you might end up adding to that list." He stopped and faced the boy. "My name is Gregori Sun."

"Darren," the boy said. "Smith."

"Right. Darren Smith. Very nice to meet you," Gregori said. The first name was real, he thought. The second not so much. "Do you have family who are looking for you, Darren Smith?"

The boy scowled and shook his head, scuffing the ground at his feet with one soggy sneaker. "No. No one cares where I am."

That, alas, had the ring of truth. Gregori thought the boy was probably a runaway from the foster system.

They dealt with plenty of those at the Blue Skies Center, unfortunately. Sometimes the system worked. Often, it did not.

He pondered the problem for a moment. He knew what Ciera would tell him to do, without even bothering to call her and ask.

"If I buy you a bus ticket in the next town, would you be willing to go to Minneapolis and visit some of my friends? You do not have to stay if the place does not suit you."

Darren pushed the hair out of his eyes and stared at him suspiciously. "What's in it for you?"

Gregori lifted one shoulder slightly. "Nothing at all. Sometimes the universe gives you an opportunity to do something for someone else. It is a gift."

"That's a pretty strange gift, man."

Gregori actually laughed out loud, something he rarely did. "You have no idea," he said. "A very strange gift indeed."

CHAPTER FOUR

ALEXEI WAS ALREADY INSIDE THE NATIONAL FOREST LANDS where Bella and Sam made their home when he stopped at a pull-off spot to eat his lunch. Over the last sixteen hours, he had traveled almost two thousand miles from Cape Cod. It would have taken almost twice that long on a non-magical motorcycle, but it was still a tiring trip, and he had worked up an appetite.

He parked the massive black Harley in the shade of a tree and delved into the fringed and studded saddlebags for the large paper bag he'd stowed there after stopping to pick up food at the convenience store he'd passed.

Alexei Knight was a giant of a man, six feet eight inches tall, wide and muscular, and he had an appetite to match his size. The bag contained two huge ham and cheese subs, a bottle of water, and two large chocolate chip cookies with nuts. It ought to hold him until he arrived at Bella's and she fed him dinner. Or maybe a late afternoon snack.

He was about to unroll the top of the bag when he thought he heard something. He cocked an ear toward the woods that lay beyond the open space where he'd parked, and the sound came again.

"Help!" a voice cried in the distance. "Help! Can anyone hear me?"

Alexei gazed mournfully at the bag in his hands and then tucked it under his arm as he took off down a hiking trail to the side of the pull-off. His huge strides ate up the distance as he jogged past trees and shrubs and one curious raccoon who looked more startled than alarmed as the huge man went thundering by.

"Hello?" Alexei called. "Hello? Where are you?"

"I'm right here, stupid," the raccoon muttered, but Alexei just waved at him and kept going.

"Hello?" the voice said. "Is somebody there? Help me! I need help!"

Alexei screeched to a halt as he almost tripped over a massive tree lying lengthwise at the edge of a clearing, still partially attached to its base. An orange chain saw lay canted on its side near the roots and a flannel-clad arm flailed around in the air not far from it. The rest of the body the arm was attached to was out of view until

Alexei stepped carefully over the tree and looked from the other side.

"Hey there," he said cheerfully to the man lying underneath the main part of the tree, partially covered by the fronds of branches. "That looks mighty uncomfortable. Are you okay?"

The man glowered at him. "No I'm not okay, you idiot. A tree fell on me!"

Alexei stroked his brown beard, still kind of missing its longer, braided length. The man on the ground had a bushy beard even darker than his, and longish graying hair that touched the top of the plaid shirt he wore. For all the yelling, the man didn't seem to be injured or bleeding, except for a couple of small scratches. From what Alexei could see, the branches were keeping most of the weight of the massive trunk from crushing the man, at least for the moment. He was, however, most definitively *stuck*. The tree was gigantic, and it was going to be nearly impossible to move it without harming the man even further.

"I can see that," Alexei said, in his usual matter-of-fact tone. There was no point in getting upset about these things. "Are you hurt? Can you tell if anything is broken?"

The man shook his head. "I hurt all over, dammit. There's a flipping tree lying on me. It's hard to breath. Damn thing is pressing right on my chest. And I've been lyin' here for hours and I'm starting to lose feeling in my legs. You've got to get me out!" A note of panic crept into his voice and he started thrashing around.

"Calm down, calm down," Alexei said. Okay, maybe there was some point to getting upset. Or at least a little worried. "I'm a lot stronger than I look, and I look plenty strong. Hang in there. I'll get this thing off of you."

The man's eyes widened until Alexei could see the whites all around the edges. "There's no way any one guy could move a tree this big. It would take a damned fork lift, and they'll never get one down this trail. I'm going to die here," he moaned. "Oh man, I'm going to die under a damn tree."

Alexei shook his head. "I'm not going to let you die. It's against my rules. Do you want me to go for help?"

"Don't leave me!" the man shrieked, his beard wobbling in the air. "I don't want to die alone!"

Alexei sighed and put down his bag of food. "Fine, fine. Let's just see how bad this is." He walked over the a place higher up on the tree where he thought he could get a good grip, and gave a mighty heave.

Fifteen minutes later, he had to admit that the answer was "Pretty damned bad." He was stronger than any three normal men put together—maybe four on a good day—but he couldn't lift the tree more than an inch or so no matter how hard he tried. Sweat running down his face and his arms were quivering with strain, but the man was still firmly pressed to the ground and his cries were getting weaker and more pitiful.

Memories flooded back as Alexei stopped to try and catch his breath. Mikhail weeping quietly in his cage, trying to keep his brothers from hearing him. Gregori groaning after a session of being bled nearly to the point of death by the insane witch that had trapped them all in a cavern deep in the woods. These woods, actually, although many miles away across the extensive lands of the National Forest. His heart skipped a beat when that thought floated through his head. Ironically, it hadn't even occurred to him before this. Now it was all he could think about.

Maybe these woods were cursed to forever thwart him. He had used all his considerable strength to try and save his brothers, and he had failed. Failed them, failed himself, failed the Baba Yagas who depended on them all, and who now had to undertake their tasks without assistance. And that had been a complicated situation, fraught with magic and trickery. This should be easier. A tree. A simple tree. But he was going to fail again. The thought was almost unendurable.

He closed his eyes and shuddered. He was about as useful as that raccoon he had passed on the trail. Maybe he could find a clan of beavers to gnaw through the tree. Except that would require a body of water nearby, and he didn't think there was one. Now he was just being ridiculous. Useless and ridiculous.

If only Mikhail was here. He could turn into that giant green monster and probably lift the tree off the man with one arm tied behind his back. Now *that* was a useful gift. Alexei's newfound talent was just the ability to talk to animals. Fun, but completely unhelpful in situations like this.

Or maybe not.

His eyes snapped open.

"Hey," the man said weakly.

"Shush," Alexei said, glancing around at the trees nearby. Finally, he saw what he was searching for—claw marks, fairly high up, deeply scratched into the bark. *Excellent.*

"Hellooo the forest," Alexei called, mentally translating his words into the necessary language. In the beginning, he hadn't even known he could do that. Then all the animals he'd ever tried to talk to, from Lulu the Great Dane to dolphins and sharks, had understood him with no problem, so it became clear he could. Thankfully, he understood them back with the same ease. "I could use a hand here. A paw, anyway."

He repeated the call a couple of times and less than five minutes later, a massive grizzly lumbered out of the forest. Its humped shoulders and long claws made it look ungainly, but Alexei knew that it could move incredibly fast if it had a reason to. The big male was probably close to eight feet tall when standing upright and could have weighed as much as seven or eight hundred pounds. Most people would have found it intimidating, but Alexei had always felt a certain kindred to bears, since he was somewhat bear-like himself.

"Good day," he called out. "Thank you for coming."

"Hello," the bear rumbled. "Who are you?"

Alexei didn't smile, since it wasn't a good idea to show your teeth to a predator, but he bent his head politely. "Greetings, sir bear. I am Alexei Knight, once the Black Rider, friend to the Baba Yagas."

The bear's short, rounded ears perked up. "I know a Baba Yaga. Her name is Bella. She is very nice. She puts out food in the winter for anyone who is hungry. Any friend of hers is welcome in my forest."

"Who are you talking to?" the man under the tree asked. "What is that sound? I can't see anything."

The bear shuffled over and sniffed at him curiously and the man gave a muffled shriek.

"Bear! There's a bear!" he said.

"Of course there is," Alexei said crossly. "I called him to help me." He turned to the bear. "I tried to lift this tree myself, but I am not strong enough. Do you think you could pick it up long enough for me to pull this Human out?"

The bear gave a chuffing laugh. "Silly Human. Should

not play with trees so large." He gave a great huffing sniff. "Human smells funny. Not right. But yes, I will help the friend of the Baba Yaga." He put both massive paws on the trunk and Alexei scooted over to stand near the man's head. As soon as the bear lifted the tree, Alexei grabbed the man's shoulders and slid him a few feet away to safety. He hoped he wasn't aggravating any injuries the man had, but there didn't seem to be much other choice.

Once the tree was back on the ground, the bear walked over to Alexei. "Silly Human," he the grizzly repeated. "Should stay out of my woods next time."

"I'll be sure to tell him," Alexei said.

"Bear," the man said weakly, and his eyes rolled back as he fainted.

Alexei snorted, sounding remarkably like his new furry friend. "I think he'll be fine," he said to the bear. "I appreciate your helping me." He trotted back to where he had dropped his lunch bag and got out the two subs. "Here. A small snack to show my gratitude."

The bear sniffed. "I smell meat and cheese. My favorites. Call any time." He took the sandwiches gently into his toothy mouth and lumbered back out of the clearing. Alexei watched his lunch leave, feeling rather wistful. But he cheered up when he remembered he still had the cookies. That was something, anyway.

Shaking his head ruefully, he turned back to the man

he had just rescued. He was checking him over when the lumberjack regained consciousness.

"You seem okay," Alexei said. "You're a lucky guy." He helped the man sit up.

"Jack," the man said, holding out one hand. "My name's Jack. Thanks for getting that tree off me. I don't understand how it happened. One minute I was cutting it down, and the next, I was pinned underneath. I probably would have died if you hadn't come along when you did." He glanced around. "Was there a bear here, or did I just hallucinate that?"

Alexei shrugged and grinned at him. "I wouldn't worry about it. You're safe now. Do you need me to call someone to come get you?"

Jack stood up gingerly, patting himself down as if to check that everything was still in the right place. He winced at a couple of places and gave a cautious cough. "I think I'm mostly just bruised. Might have cracked a rib or two, but all things considered, I think I got off pretty easy. The branches on the underside mostly kept the weight of the tree off me, even though I couldn't move."

He pointed further down the trail. "My truck's not far from here on an access road. I should be okay to get back to it and drive home."

"If you're sure," Alexei said. "You must be feeling a little shaky after all that."

"Just hungry," Jack said. "I'll be fine when I get something to eat and drink."

Alexei handed over the bag in his hand reluctantly. "There's water and a couple of big cookies in there. But I'd get checked out just in case."

He watched Jack limp off with the rest of his lunch, but a sense of satisfaction eventually overtook the regret over his lost food. It felt good to be able to use his new gift to help someone, the way he had when he'd worked with Beka to find and stop a dragon-turned-pirate back in Cape Cod. Alexei loved his new life with Bethany; what's not to like about living with a beautiful woman, and helping to run a bar? But he had to admit to himself that occasionally he missed the adventures he used to have with his brothers and the Baba Yagas.

Brenna had stolen a lot more than their immortality from the three of them, and moments like this one were few and far between. Still, it had been fun. Well, probably not for Jack, but it all worked out okay.

Alexei walked slowly back to his Harley, savoring the resinous smells of the woods and the chatter of gossiping squirrels. He wondered if Mikhail and Gregori would show up at Bella's. Then he smiled. At least he had a good story to tell them if they did.

CHAPTER FIVE

Mikhail pulled his white Yamaha into the large dirt clearing that doubled as a driveway for Bella and Sam's cabin in the Wyoming woods. Beka's colorfully painted converted school bus was parked next to Barbara's gleaming silver Airstream, but his was the only motorcycle, so clearly his brothers weren't here yet. Or weren't coming at all, as he'd predicted.

He didn't bother to put down the kickstand, since his enchanted steed could stay upright perfectly well without it when there were no nosy Humans to question the impossibility. He hadn't even grabbed his white leather saddlebags before the front door of the cabin burst open and what seemed like a torrent of people flowed out.

After a flurry of hugging (and a friendly punch on the shoulder from Barbara, who wasn't the hugging type, and after all, had seen him recently), the crowd resolved itself into its composite parts. Fiery-haired Bella stood with her husband Sam, his formerly vivid burn scars barely visible, and gave Mikhail a smile as bright as her tresses. Beka grinned at him, her willowy blond California surfer-girl good looks belying the strength that allowed her to swim with the dolphins for hours or take on a modern-day pirate who threatened to pollute her beloved ocean.

Barbara, beautiful and fierce with her slightly long nose and wild cloud of dark hair, simply nodded her head. Little Babs stood next to her wearing her usual solemn expression, although her eyes sparkled at the sight of her friend from home.

Only one person stood apart from the rest, gazing at him shyly from under shaggy bangs that edged into equally shaggy brown hair that was longer than when he'd seen it last. The turquoise blue streak was new. Of course, everything about Jazz was different. Insanely, impossibly different.

After all his years of traveling with the Baba Yagas, and in and out of the fantastical Otherworld, you'd think he would have grown accustomed to the impossible. Yet nothing he'd ever seen compared to this. He'd heard what happened, of course, but knowing about it and seeing the reality with his own eyes were two completely different things.

"Jazz?" he said. "Is that you?"

The first time he'd met Bella's apprentice was when she had helped to rescue him and his brothers from the evil Brenna. At that point Jazz was just a teenage runaway from the foster system. She got caught up in the whole dramatic affair only to discover that not only was the magic she'd always dreamed of true, but that she had an amazingly powerful innate talent for it.

In the end, the High Queen of the Otherworld had granted Bella permission to train Jazz to take up an extra position as a Baba Yaga. As Barbara had pointed out, the Human world was growing more complicated every day, and the existing witches were having a tough time keeping up with the Human-created imbalances in nature. Adding another Baba seemed like a sensible move.

Jazz had spent a brief time with the Riders after they had been freed from Brenna's torture. They had been in terrible shape, both physically and mentally, and Mikhail had only a vague and disjointed memory of the raga-muffin teen Bella had taken in after she'd found the girl living alone in the forest. Then he'd seen Jazz again almost a year later, when Bella and Sam brought her to Mikhail's wedding.

But that girl had been sixteen, and the woman standing in front of him now looked more like she was in her mid-to-late twenties. Only her brown eyes looked the same, wide and clear and wary, the eyes of someone who has seen much more cruelty and evil than she should have, no matter what age she was.

Not long after the wedding, Jazz had attempted an ambitious spell to give the Riders back their immortality. A noble aim, but one which had backfired badly, causing the girl to age ten years in an instant, nearly killing her. Bella had arrived in time to save Jazz's life, but the damage was done. The queen had declared Jazz too powerful to be allowed to continue to live on the Human side of the doorway without more training, and ordered both her and Bella to spend a year in the Otherworld so that Bella could provide the girl with an intensive course in how to be a Baba Yaga.

Now they were home at last, and the adult version of Jazz stared back at him, biting her lip from underneath her fringe of brown hair.

"Hi Mikhail," she said in a quiet voice. "It's nice to see you again. How are Jenna and the baby doing?" She gave a barely visible wince. "Sorry. I guess she's not a baby anymore, is she?"

Mikhail smiled at her, bringing all his not-inconsider-able charm to bear to try and set her at ease. "Flora is doing great," he said. "She's starting to walk and getting into everything. You'll have to come visit. Jenna would love to see you again."

This earned him a hesitant smile in return. "Thanks,"

Jazz said. "I'd like that." She glanced over his shoulder. "Um, are your brothers coming? I know Bella invited them."

Mikhail shrugged, not wanting to show how much their absence cut to his core. It was a pain he'd grown accustomed to, but it never stopped gnawing at his soul. "Honestly, your guess is as good as mine. They've always been a tad unpredictable."

At Barbara's side, her dragon Chudo-Yudo, (in his guise as a giant white pit bull), gave a snort. Tiny sparks shot out of his broad black nose. "That's an understatement," he said.

Chewie, Beka's dragon, who looked (for the moment, anyway) like a huge ebony Newfoundland, nodded in agreement. "We had a running wager on which one of you would show up first."

"Or at all," Bella's Norwegian Forest Cat-dragon added, looking as disgruntled as any true cat deprived of a treat. "I had my money on none of you coming."

Mikhail hid a grin behind one hand as he pretended to cough. It didn't to do piss off the dragon-cat. He had sharp claws in either form. "Sorry about that, Koshka. I'll try to make it up to you. I might have slipped a couple of cans of tuna into my saddlebags before leaving the house."

Koshka perked up. "I suppose I'll forgive you, then," he said.

"I'm not sure any of you is going to win that bet," Barbara said, nodding in the direction of the long dirt road that led to the cabin. The distant rumble of powerful engines grew closer as a black Harley and a red Ducati came into view. "For which I am immensely grateful."

A weight he didn't know he'd been carrying seemed to lift off of Mikhail's shoulders at the sight of the two motorcycles and the cargo they carried. His heart beat so fast, he could feel it pulsing against his ribs. He couldn't have said if it was from excitement or nerves at the thought of finally reuniting with his brothers after all this time.

The bikes came to a halt in front of the group already standing there. A massive form dismounted from the Harley and lifted its helmet to reveal the slightly changed but still familiar face of his middle half-brother.

"Hey there," Alexei said, as calmly as if he arrived at such a gathering every day. "Look what I found a short way down the road."

Gregori pulled off his own helmet and bowed in the general direction of the Baba Yagas, acknowledging Mikhail with a nod and an out-of-character wink. "May anyone join this party?" he asked. "I brought the makings for s'mores."

Chewie wagged his black tail so hard, dust sprang up around him. "S'mores. Excellent."

"You shaved off your mustache," Mikhail said to his oldest brother. Gregori looked different without the Fu Manchu he'd sported for centuries in honor of his Mongolian roots, although his calm demeanor hadn't changed. "And you cut your beard, Alexei. It's almost...neat."

"Bethany thought the long braided beard made me look like a cross between an out of work Viking and a troll," Alexei growled. "Apparently that's a bad thing. Go figure."

Beka laughed, the sound a merry note in the too-tense clearing. "You're not fooling anyone, Alexei," she said. "You would have dyed it purple if Bethany asked you to. You're wild about the woman." She could sound so certain since the blond Baba Yaga had been around to witness their budding romance, which started while Alexei fought pirates, a kraken, and his own inner demons.

"Ha!" Alexei retorted. "Shows what you know. I *like* purple." He turned to peruse Mikhail. "You haven't changed at all, brother, although it is strange to see you wearing something other than white."

All the brothers had given up their trademark colors —white for Mikhail, red for Gregori, and black for Alexei—when they'd stopped being the White Rider, the Red Rider, and the Black Rider. Apparently the others had found it just as painful as Mikhail had to stick to the clothes they'd worn so long for a role they no longer had.

Mikhail noted that they all had on nearly identical outfits—black leather jackets, jeans, motorcycle boots, and variously hued shirts. He wore a vivid blue denim that matched his eyes, Gregori's was green silk with a matching leather cord that held back his long tail of black hair, and Alexei had on a white tee with the symbol of a pirate's hook crossing an anchor which said "Sail in to The Hook and Anchor for a dangerously good time."

"We have all changed," Mikhail said with a shrug. "How could we not, when nothing about our lives is the same anymore?"

The three of them stood around for a moment, awkward after their long separation, and none of them seeming to know what to do next.

Chudo-Yudo cleared his throat in a vaguely threatening way and showed them all a mouthful of gleaming white teeth. "This is a damned reunion," he said. "If I don't see some hugging in the next two minutes, I'm going to bite someone."

Jazz smothered a laugh, her brown eyes suspiciously bright.

Alexei was the first to break. He had always been the most openly emotional of the brothers, with everything he thought or felt right there on the surface. He wrapped one massive arm around Mikhail and the other around

Gregori and lifted them off the ground in a huge bear hug. All the brothers were tall and strong, but Alexei dwarfed the others. It was not for nothing that he'd been called a one-man army, or a walking mountain, and he held them up with ease as they squirmed.

"Put me down, you big oaf," Gregori finally said with an affectionate if somewhat aggravated note in his voice.

"Seriously, dude," Mikhail added his protests. But he hugged both brothers hard for a second after his feet touched the earth again. "I'd almost forgotten how big you were."

"As if anyone could forget that," Barbara said briskly. But Mikhail was pretty sure he'd seen her dash away a rare tear.

"It is so good to see you all together again," Bella said. "I don't suppose any of you are hungry?"

Three heads nodded in unison, and Alexei added predictably, "And thirsty. I don't suppose you have any beer? Or vodka. Vodka's good too."

A couple of hours later they were all sitting around on lawn chairs in a circle, with the two younger girls (and the dragon-dogs and cat) perched on the ground, having just finished off an excellent barbeque prepared by Bella. If anyone noticed that Sam still stayed a little further back from the fire than the rest of them, no one commented on it.

The brothers were finally feeling more at ease with each other, and Gregori thought that they had *almost* adjusted to the transformed Jazz. Babs had spent the meal shifting around the group to sit by each Rider in turn, not saying much as usual, but clearly happy to have them all together.

"Does it feel odd to be an adult instead of a teen?" Alexei finally asked Jazz in his usual blunt fashion. His third, or possibly fourth, beer dangled from his large hand, but with his size and unusually tough constitution, it was unlikely he even noticed.

Bella snorted. "Don't let the outside fool you. She's still a teenager on the inside, at least part of the time."

"As if," Jazz said, rolling her eyes. Gregori rather thought that proved Bella's point, but he decided not to say so.

"Even if I hadn't magicked myself older, I'd be seventeen now," she said. "That's practically an adult. But yeah, it is still a little weird to look in the mirror and see all this staring back at me." She waved one hand from her older face down her changed body.

"We are all very sorry this happened while you were attempting a spell intended to help us," Gregori said. "It was kind of you to try, but we would never have wanted you to take such a risk on our behalves."

Jazz scrunched up her face in a scowl. "Right, unlike the risks you and Mikhail and Alexei undertook on behalf of the Baba Yagas through the years." She dropped her eyes to the ground. "I'm only sorry I failed you.

"But hey," she said, perking up a little, "after spending a year doing all this uber-training with Bella, I am way more skilled now, so maybe I could take what I've learned and try again."

"*NO!!!*" Everyone else in the clearing shouted in unison.

"Jeez, you guys, overreact much?" Jazz said.

Bella, who was sitting as close to her husband as possible, banged her head against Sam's broad shoulder. "Argh," she said. "You might have put ten years on your life that day, but you took ten years off of mine. If you ever even think about trying that kind of spell again, I'm going to lock you in your room for a month; I don't care how old you are."

"Jeez," her apprentice said again, but a small smile played at the corner of her lips. After spending most of her earlier years in abusive or indifferent foster homes, Gregori suspected that Jazz secretly liked the fact that someone cared enough to worry about her, no matter how annoying it might be.

Sam gave her a serious look, holding on to Bella's hand as though she might vanish for another year. The queen had allowed Bella and Jazz to visit him briefly a number of times during their stint in the Otherworld, but it had still been rough on the couple, who were practically newlyweds. "Jazz, I think everyone appreciates how much you want to help the Riders, but maybe you should ask them if they even want their immortality back again."

"What?" Jazz's eyes opened wide. "Why wouldn't they want it? Brenna stole their immortality from them. Of course they want it returned so they can go back to being who they were."

Gregori exchanged glances with his brothers, Mikhail and Alexei nodding in silent agreement with the truth they could see in his eyes.

"I do not believe we would wish for such a thing, even if it were possible," Gregori said. "We have all built new lives for ourselves, and found happiness with Human women. *Mortal* Human women," he stressed. "If you were able to return our immortality, it would change everything."

"I think we're mostly content the way we are," Alexei agreed, lifting his beer in a salute to his brothers, who raised their own in agreement. "I like helping to run the bar and talking to the local ocean creatures. And I wouldn't give up Bethany for another thousand years of life without her."

Mikhail smiled at Jazz. "You may be ten years older in body, and another year older in experience, not to mention being one of the most powerful natural witches who has come along in centuries, but you have a lot left to learn about the real world. Yes, there was a time when we probably would have given just about anything to go back to who we were. But things are different now."

"Oh," Jazz said in a quiet voice. "But don't you miss being the Riders?"

Gregori heard something unspoken behind her words, and had a momentary ping from his precognitive sense. But as often happened, he could not quite pin down what it was. "Of course we do," he said. "It was why we were created, and from time to time, no matter how satisfying our current existence might be, I suspect we all feel the drive to take to the road and find a Baba Yaga to help. But that part of our lives is in the past now."

"Well," Barbara said, a sly smile curving up her lips on one side. "We might just have a solution to that, if you still want one."

"What are you talking about?" Alexei asked, sounding as confused as Gregori felt.

The other two Baba Yagas were openly grinning now, and they all turned to gaze in the direction of Barbara's Airstream. As the Riders looked on in amazement, the door opened and the slim, upright form of the High Queen of the Otherworld descended gracefully down the steps as if she was walking into her own palace instead of a dusty clearing in front of a simple cabin in the woods.

Gregori could not remember the last time the queen had crossed through the doorway to this world. He was not certain it had happened even once since she ordered all the paranormals who could leave their earthly environments to relocate permanently to the Otherworld to escape the encroaching Humans. The unexpected sight was clearly a shock to his brothers as well. Alexei's mouth hung open and the normally suave Mikhail wavered for a moment before he sprang to his feet. Gregori kicked Alexei none-too-gently on the shin to remind him of his manners, then all three rose to walk over to the queen and bow down on one knee before her.

"Your Majesty," Mikhail said. "This is an unexpected honor."

The queen looked as magnificent as usual, although she was marginally dressed down from her usual court attire. Her gown was an impossible variety of blue and green hues crafted from multiple layers of the finest silk, so that when she moved it was as though she was every shade of the ocean flowing together at once, but it lacked her usual train and wide skirts. Her gleaming silver-white hair was twisted into braids that had been bound up with beads of blue topaz, sapphire, and peridot, and then piled atop her head. The gems glittered in the fading sunlight, but not as much as her usual diamond and amethyst tiara would have done. Matching jewels hung around her swanlike neck and dangled from her delicate ears.

As always, her beauty was almost too much to behold, but Gregori suspected that this was her version of "roughing it." He was honored and touched, as well as a little bit amused, although he was careful not to let any hint of the latter cross his face.

"It is wonderful to see you all together again at last," the queen said. She stood before each man in turn, briefly resting one slim white hand on his shoulder before giving them each a light kiss on the cheek and indicating that they should rise.

It was both a blessing and a benediction, and Gregori felt it resonate down to his toes. Given the stunned look on both his brothers' faces, he had no doubt they felt the same. It was a singular honor from a singular monarch.

"Goodness," the queen said, looking up at them. "We always forget how tall you are. This won't do at all." She always spoke in the royal "We," of course. "Perhaps someone might fetch me a chair?"

Bella had already sent Sam scurrying into the house, and he returned carrying a tall stool with a scrolled metal back on it. "I'm sorry, Your Majesty," he said with a small bow. "I'm afraid it is the best we have. We don't usually entertain royalty."

The queen raised one silvery eyebrow and looked around at the parked vehicles, and the portable copper fire pit they'd all been sitting around on a motley assortment of lawn and camping chairs.

"One does get that feeling," she said with just the suggestion of a smile. "But no matter. It is easily enough remedied." She waved a hand languidly and the stool shimmered, transforming itself into an even higher chair made of ebony and wrought iron, covered with intricate designs. Two small steps lead up to it that might or might not have been carved from blocks of obsidian. She climbed them with her usual dignity, holding her skirts up out of her way and then arranging them effortlessly as she sat down on what now looked suspiciously like a throne.

"Ah, that is better," she said, looking down at the three Riders instead of up. She aimed vivid purple eyes pointedly in Bella's direction. "So. We see that We have interrupted a party. What are you all drinking?"

Bella flushed, clearly feeling as though she had underprepared for a visit by such a grand monarch. "Uh, beer, Your Majesty. It's a very nice one that is brewed locally, but I don't know if it would be to your tastes. I could go fetch a bottle of wine, if you like."

The queen gave an unexpectedly wistful smile. "Beer. A wizard from Chicago once visited Us and brought a gift of beer crafted by a man named Mac. It was quite delightful. We would be pleased to taste another. The wines of the Otherworld are most agreeable, but even their perfection can become tedious over the centuries. We might enjoy a change of pace."

Sam hurriedly uncapped another beer and handed it to Bella, who looked at the plain brown bottle uncertainly. Barbara stepped up and plucked it from her grasp. "Allow me," the eldest Baba Yaga said. She snapped her fingers and a golden goblet appeared from thin air, no doubt procured from her Airstream. She poured the beer into it and handed it to the queen with a flourish. "Your ale, Your Majesty."

Everyone held their breath while the queen took a small sip. "Delightful," she pronounced. "Now, to the reason for my visit." She turned her attention back to the Riders.

"You are all looking quite well. We are pleased to see that this is so, even if," and here she gave them all a stern but not entirely convincing scowl, "even if We had to make a pilgrimage here to see it for Ourselves."

She ignored their murmured apologies. "It is no matter. I understand that each of you had built a new life for yourself out of the ruins of the old." She gazed fondly at Alexei. "We are told you own a tavern now. How astonishingly suitable."

Alexei grinned at her, as usual the least intimidated by her power and glory. Luckily, she seemed to like that about him, since she had so far refrained from turning him into a toad.

"Isn't it, though?" he said. "The bar belongs to my wife's father, a former fisherman. But he's in a wheelchair and can't handle the place on his own, so Bethany runs it and I help out from time to time."

"If by help, you mean, toss people out when they get too rowdy, and carry heavy beer kegs around," Beka muttered under her breath.

"Hey!" Alexei protested. "I also walk the dogs."

The queen's amethyst stare swung to Chudo-Yudo and Chewie and then back to Alexei. "You have dogs?"

"Dog dogs," Alexei clarified. "Not dragon-dogs. Nothing magical about them, unless you count the amount of food they can make disappear. They're Great Danes."

"Ah," the queen said, and turned to Gregori. "And do you have a dog as well?"

"Indeed, I do not," Gregori responded. He thought dogs were mostly large and messy, rather like his brother Alexei, if one considered it. "My wife Ciera and I have a black cat named Magic." He nodded at Koshka. "The cat is not, in fact, magical either."

The queen pursed her perfect rose-colored lips. "But you are happy?

He bowed, hands folded in front of his chest. "I am, Your Majesty. Ciera founded a center for troubled youth, and I am pleased to assist her with such a worthwhile endeavor. Mostly I teach classes on self-defense and meditation, although I will turn my hands to anything that needs to be done."

The queen shifted on her not-throne. "And you, Mikhail Day. You have an infant, do you not? The child of your Human mate?" She gave a tiny shrug. "We do not recall her name, alas."

Mikhail swept down in a showier bow that his brother had given. "My wife's name is Jenna, Majesty, and her daughter—our daughter—is named Flora." He gave the queen a rueful smile. "I'm afraid she is more a toddler than an infant, these days. Less random noise, more chaos. But a delight, none the less."

A dainty sigh floated upward like an iridescent soap bubble. "One forgets how quickly things move on this side of the doorway," the queen said with something like regret. "Do bring the child to visit Us again soon." She looked around the semi-circle of Riders in front of her. "In fact, it is Our wish that you should all visit Us soon, now that you have recovered from your ordeal."

Those purple eyes seemed to pierce Gregori's soul, and he suspected they had the same effect on his brothers, as the queen stared at each of them for a long moment. "You *have* recovered, have you not?"

"As much as will ever be possible, Your Majesty," Gregori answered for them all. "We have adjusted to our new circumstances, and we are content."

"Happy, even," Mikhail said, and Alexei nodded. "It's a

good life," he said. "I can drink all the beer I want. *Free*." Everyone chuckled.

"So, there is nothing more you want?" the queen asked. "You are completely satisfied with your lot? There is no boon you would ask from Us, if given the chance?" She took a delicate sip of beer from her goblet as if she had no great interest in the answer to the question she had just posed. But the way the gathered Baba Yagas shifted restlessly made Gregori think the inquiry might not be as casual as it seemed.

Alexei shuffled his feet, staring at the ground and saying nothing. Mikhail cleared his throat, started to speak, and then fell silent again. Finally, Gregori took a step forward, as reluctant to put his feelings into words as his brothers clearly were.

"We all miss being the Riders," he said. "It was why our father, the god Jarilo, created us, after all. We are driven to help on some level that is probably wrapped like a primordial snake around our DNA. But we have found other ways to satisfy that drive, even if they might not be as glamorous as being the companions to the most powerful witches in the world. It is not the same, but then, nothing is. And we are well aware that nothing can be done to change this." He stared pointedly at Jazz. "Nor would we wish to go back."

The queen tapped her lips thoughtfully. "But what if you could go forward?"

CHAPTER SIX

"Forward?" Alexei thought he might need another beer or three before this conversation made any sense. He glanced at Gregori, but even the smartest of the brothers seemed to be as baffled as he was. "Of course we are going forward. That's the only direction to go in."

"Shush, Alexei," Barbara said. "Let the queen speak."

He shushed. Alexei had no desire to become a swan or a piece of statuary.

The queen took another sip of beer and sat back a little on her almost-certainly-not-a-throne, which thoughtfully produced a pillow exactly where it was needed.

"As you are no doubt aware, Bella and her apprentice Jazz have spent much of the last year in a quiet corner of the Otherworld, where Jazz could get the intensive training that her unusually strong powers clearly required." A chilly amethyst glance swept over the pair before the queen went on. "But before they left to return to this side of the doorway, young Jazz approached me with a request."

Jazz, who had been hovering at the edge of the circle formed by the three Riders and the queen, cleared her throat. "More of a suggestion than a request, really," she said. It could be unwise to ask or owe a favor in the Otherworld.

The queen hid a small smile behind one pale hand. "Indeed. As you say. A suggestion."

Mikhail looked as baffled as Alexei felt, which made Alexei feel marginally better. "What was the suggestion, Your Majesty? Did it have something to do with us?"

"It did indeed," the queen said. "Perhaps the young lady would care to explain it to you herself." She beckoned Jazz forward.

"It wasn't really a big deal," Jazz said, her normally sallow cheeks flushing. "We went to see the queen and her consort before we came home. I might have mentioned that I would have felt better about setting out on my first solo job as a Baba Yaga if I knew I had the Riders to call on if things got rough, like all the Baba Yagas who came before me."

"We wish you had that too, little one," Alexei said. He loved Bethany more than anything, and had no desire to leave her or the dogs or the bar. But still, there were days when the wind seemed to call his name and even his enchanted Harley felt restless underneath him. "But we are the Riders no more. The queen herself said so, when we lost our immortality. And all the wishes in the world can't change that."

"Ah," Jazz said, lifting one finger into the air. "But the queen can."

"What?" Mikhail said, the blood rushing from his face until he was almost as pale as the white shirts he used to wear. "What are you talking about, Jazz?"

Jazz bit her lip. "I just pointed out to Her Majesty that while you might not be immortal anymore, you were still way stronger and smarter and" (here she looked directly at Mikhail) "more charming than regular Humans. Plus you all have your new abilities, which might be kind of handy when dealing with paranormal issues. And I suggested that just because you had created satisfying lives didn't mean you might not want to help out occasionally, if one of us really needed it. Or, you know, if you were like, bored or something."

Alexei, who had an extremely low boredom threshold, perked up immediately. "You mean you asked if we could go back to being the Riders, only part-time?"

All three heads—blond, brown, and black—swiveled toward the queen.

"Your Majesty?" Gregori asked, looking as though he

was thinking furiously. Or holding his breath. Or both. "It that even possible?"

The queen pursed her lips. "Almost anything is possible, should one decide to make it so. Not everything, but almost." She drained her goblet and handed it back to Barbara. "Therefore, We decided to entertain her proposal."

"And?" Alexei asked, practically dancing from one foot to the other in his eagerness to hear the answer. Gregori's stillness had taken on a nearly preternatural quality, and Mikhail had put his hands behind his back and was clasping them together so hard, Alexei thought he heard a knuckle pop.

The queen raised an eyebrow, as if to tell him to curb his eagerness. "*And* We decided that We were prepared to consider the idea. But only after putting each of you to a test, as is traditional, to see if you were truly able to move past the traumas you had been through. Additionally, We wished to determine if you were capable of using your new gifts in ways that would be useful to the roles you had once fulfilled, and willing to risk your personal safety even if you were no longer immortal."

Tests. The word rang through Alexei's brain. *Sonofabitch. Freaking traditional fairy tale tests. That explained a lot.*

"The pregnant woman whose child was lost in a cave!" Mikhail exclaimed, at the exact same time Gregori said,

"The boy on the bridge who jumped!" and Alexei said, a little indignantly, "That crabby guy stuck under the tree!"

Bella and Beka laughed, Jazz giggled, and even the normally stern Barbara cracked a smile. Little Babs looked as solemn as usual, but there might have been a twinkle in her bright brown eyes. Only Sam looked confused, and Alexei had a sneaking suspicion that all the women in the clearing had been in on this, whatever *this* was.

The queen inclined her head gracefully, the gemstones bound within her braids reflecting the last of the setting sun's rays and giving her the illusion of a halo Alexei was beginning to think she didn't deserve. "Indeed, those encounters were arranged by Us, to test your will, determination, ingenuity, and heart."

"You put all those people at risk simply to test us?" Gregori said in a low, dangerous tone. Barbara reached out and put a calming hand on his arm.

"Not at all," the queen said. "You know We try to avoid interactions with Humans as much as is possible. Besides, it was unnecessary. All those who you met upon your travels were My people, who I glamoured to appear Human and vulnerable.

"But they were never in any danger. The 'small child' you rescued was actually a gnome who was perfectly comfortable underground. Gregori's suicidal teen was a nixie; as a water creature, he would not have drowned even if Gregori had not jumped in after him. As for Alexei's grumpy woodcutter, that was a tough dryad who could have lain under that tree all day and half the night and never been harmed. Although doing so would likely not have improved his disposition."

"No wonder the bear said he smelled funny," Alexei muttered under his breath.

The queen gave the tiniest hint of a smile. "Not that We ever truly doubted you would come to their rescue, even so.

"Do not be displeased with My creatures, who were merely doing as they had been bid. Nor with Us, since it was necessary to be certain if you were still Riders at heart, despite all that had occurred."

Mikhail let out a gusty sigh, then shook himself, as if letting go of some shadow that had been clinging to him like beads of water to the surface of a leaf. "You are wise as always, Your Majesty," he said with a bow. "To be honest, before your test, I would not have been so sure of my willingness to help another damsel in distress, or if I had the courage to deliberately enter a dark cave. Nor had I ever attempted to call up my beast on purpose, to utilize the abilities he has that I do not. No matter what happens, I am grateful."

"As am I," Gregori said, looking thoughtful.

Alexei shrugged and rolled his eyes. As far as he was concerned, it was all a big fuss over nothing. What really mattered was whether or not the queen thought her experiment was a success. He could almost feel the road under his wheels again, close enough to their impossible dream that he could taste it.

"Did we pass?" he demanded. "Are you going to do what Jazz asked and make us Riders again?"

The three men each took an unconscious step closer to each other, as if they could gather strength from the others as they waited for the answer to Alexei's question. For a moment, the clearing was so silent, even the sound of their own breathing seemed too loud. An owl hooted in a nearby tree and made Alexei jump.

"Most definitely," the queen said with an affectionate smile. "You all passed the tests We set you. From the reports We received, you were quite remarkable. Not that this comes as any surprise. If you so desire, and if your mates are agreeable, you may once again be called The Riders—White, Red, and Black—and assist the Baba Yagas when there is a need and you can be spared from your regular lives."

Everyone in the clearing cheered: the three established Baba Yagas, their various Chudo-Yudos, Sam, and even Babs, who was not given to displays of exuberance. But Jazz cheered the loudest of all, jumping up and down and waving one arm through the air while making "whoop whoop whoop" noises. It reminded Alexei of a silly romantic movie Beka had once made him watch.

Only a firm glance from Bella finally brought the newest Baba Yaga back down to earth.

The three brothers bowed at once, first at the queen, then in the direction of each of the Baba Yagas. "We would be honored," Gregori said in a formal tone, speaking for them all. "Our lives may now be measured in decades rather than centuries, but we would be grateful to spend some of those days being of service to Your Majesty and those who do her work on this side of the doorway."

The queen looked unaccustomedly misty-eyed as she gazed around at them all. "It is We who are honored to accept that service," she said. "You were broken for a time by your terrible experiences at the hands of That Person, whose name We no longer speak, and by the losses that followed. But you all triumphed in the end, building new lives and finding true love, and you are broken no longer. Once you were Riders by design and destiny; now you are Riders by choice. We are most pleased."

She arose from her chair and moved to each man in turn, giving him a kiss on the forehead. Alexei could feel the magic tingling through his bones as her cool lips touched his skin.

"Good journeying to you all," she said as she moved toward the door of the Airstream. "And may your travels bring you to visit Us at court soon."

The clearing seemed somehow smaller and quieter

after she left, although fireflies appeared in the twilight air around them, feasting on the traces of leftover magic.

"Well, that went better than I'd hoped," Barbara said in her usual brisk voice, although she pulled out a handkerchief and blew her nose into it, which rather ruined the illusion. "Nicely done, all three of you."

Alexei shook his head. "I don't think we deserve any of the credit," he said. "But I know who does." He strolled over to Jazz where she stood beaming next to Bella, and gave her a huge hug that nearly cracked her spine. "Thank you, Jazz. You might not have been able to give us back our immortality, but in a way, this is even better."

"It is all we truly wanted," Gregori said, following him over and giving Jazz a bow so low, his head nearly touched the ground. "You did well. None of the rest of us even considered the possibility of such a compromise, yet you were smart enough and bold enough to suggest it to the queen."

Mikhail hugged her too, and then kissed the top of her head. "I think you're going to make one hell of a Baba Yaga."

Jazz sniffled and wiped her eyes. "You're just saying that because you get to be the Riders again."

"They're saying it because it is true," Bella said, putting one arm around her protégé. "You may give me gray hairs with the way you think outside the box and refuse to give up in the face of reasonable facts, but maybe that kind of attitude is just what the Baba Yagas need."

"What the world needs," Beka said, grinning. "You're going to kick ass and take names."

"Hey, that's *my* job," Barbara said. "Although I guess there are enough asses in need of kicking to go around."

Alexei grabbed his beer from where he'd put it down when the queen had showed up so unexpectedly. "I'd like to propose a toast," he said, raising his drink high in the air. "To new adventures!"

"To new adventures!" everyone echoed him, raising their drinks too (even Babs with her glass of milk).

As Alexei took a long swallow, he noticed something that no one else did, perhaps because he was standing the closest to Gregori.

The oldest Rider was staring at Barbara with an odd expression on his normally serene face, as if he were seeing something not visible to the rest. "Oh dear," Gregori said quietly. "New adventures. Uh oh."

ABOUT THE AUTHOR

Deborah Blake is the award-winning author of the Baba Yaga and Broken Rider paranormal romance series and the Veiled Magic urban fantasies from Berkley. Deborah has also written The Goddess is in the Details, Everyday Witchcraft and numerous other books from Llewellyn, along with a popular tarot deck. She has published articles in Llewellyn annuals, and her ongoing column, "Everyday Witchcraft" is featured in Witches & Pagans Magazine. Deborah can be found online at Facebook, Twitter, her popular blog (Writing the Witchy Way), and www.deborahblakeauthor.com

When not writing, Deborah runs The Artisans' Guild, a cooperative shop she founded with a friend in 1999, and also works as a jewelry maker, tarot reader, and energy healer. She lives in a 130 year old farmhouse in rural upstate New York with various cats who supervise all her activities, both magickal and mundane.

CPSIA information can be obtained
at www.ICGtesting.com
Printed in the USA
LVHW090324110221
678967LV00001B/46

9 781717 903341